CARNAL
DARKNESS

CARNAL
DARKNESS

by

Andrew Zepherin Wallace

ANONYMOUS EYE

Published by Anonymous Eye

ANONYMOUS EYE

ISBN 978-1-9991523-0-7

Cover art, *Everwolf* © Paul Duncan

Printed and bound in Canada

Ordering Information:
Special discounts are available on quantity purchases by corporations,
associations, educators, and others.

The author welcomes you to contact him at andrew.z.wallace@gmail.com

for

my wife

I

I SLAM THE DOOR ON LAURA'S YELLING AND MAKE HASTE towards Chinatown. Once again, a vicious argument has erupted over nothing. And, as a result, it's either leave alone, take her along with me to awkwardly charade among friends, or else stay home until senseless anger finds expression in domestic violence. Yes, our relationship is a festering, toxic mess. That's not to say, however, that it's entirely void of love. On the contrary, love frequently shows its face. It's just that, when it does, it tends to be tear-streaked.

Earlier that day, we had agreed to do Chinese food at George's. His home and ours are situated at opposite ends of Chinatown, so feasting on dumplings and chow mien is a regular occurrence. If it had been a proper occasion of some kind, a birthday or a baptism, I would've insisted on Laura being present. But, since it's just spontaneous noodles among friends, her absence can easily be excused.

This time, the burden is on me to select the dishes. But I already know what to order, and I know exactly where to order from—a place called Duck Son, our decided favorite because of its cheap beer and unique fortune cookies.

With anger fueling my gait, I arrive at the restaurant in record time and make my way down its grimy steps and through its plastic, strip-curtain door. Near the entrance hangs a shrine dedicated to the red-faced Guan Yu and, on the back wall, a television. Aside from these two fixtures, pictures of menu items cover almost every inch of the grease- and smoke-stained walls. Evidently, it is by means of this display that patrons unable to speak some form of Chinese can still communicate what they wish to consume. A large poster board positioned near the front counter serves precisely the same purpose. They have a menu, of course, but the translations are all pinyin and gibberish. Without such visuals, ordering is a mere shot in the dark.

The woman at the front counter is heavyset with tight, black curls and a face caked with so much makeup that she would look at home as a Lao Dan in a Beijing opera. Recognizing me, she smiles and motions to the poster board. I confidently point to Kung Pao chicken, pan-fried dumplings, chow mien, and fried rice— selecting vegetarian options where applicable. Katie, George's roommate, is a herbivore. And, because of

Laura, I am an on-again, off-again vegetarian myself, but, with her brooding in the apartment, Kung Pao chicken is a no-brainer. As somewhat of an afterthought, I order a plate of mapo tofu as well. Personally, I find the stuff disgusting, but George is crazy about it. Besides, I'd better order an extra dish in case his other roommate, Kelly, is around.

The Lao Dan behind the counter nods her head with each selection and scribbles out a list on receipt paper. Her notes complete, she poorly pronounces the word "fifteen" and smacks the head of a golden beckoning cat clutching a digital clock on the counter. The numbers read ten to six, so I understand her "fifteen" to mean that the food will be ready either in fifteen minutes or at fifteen after. Whichever, I have time to kill. I contemplate ordering a beer, but, with one look at the Sino soap being aired on the wall-mounted television, I decide to wait outside.

Directly above Duck Son is a "massage" parlour. Indeed, the sign out front—complete with an unusually large-breasted, sud-covered woman and the words "FREE SHOWER"—indicate that more than massages are available. I sit down on one of the steps leading up to the place and light a smoke.

Chinatown is crowded as usual—a mix of races bustling about, buying, selling, consuming. No bars, unfortunately. I'd like a beer, but the only places that serve alcohol are restaurants and KTVs. For whatever reason, the folks around here aren't too hepped up on Western-style drinking establishments—loud, flashy clubs aside, that is. But Chinatown is no place for clubs; it's all food, cheap goods, and karaoke. A club wouldn't fit. Besides, above most of the businesses in the district are residences, and Chinatown is already several decibels above average.

As if to accentuate my point, a man on the opposite side of the road starts screaming through a megaphone. "FALUN DAFA GOOOOD!" he shouts. "CPC BAAAAD!" He and a few others are marching about with pamphlets that I've no doubt been handed on previous occasions. I know the group, and their publications are all alike. They inevitably explain that Falun Gong is nothing more than a meditation and self-cultivation practice based on the principles of truthfulness, compassion, and forbearance, which together constitute the fundamental nature of the cosmos. Various exercises, such as "Buddha Stretching a Thousand Arms" and "Penetrating the Cosmic Extremes" are depicted, and the remaining space is normally devoted to a discussion of the unjust persecution of Falun Gong in the People's Republic of China.

Today, the group is also equipped with a banner. Even from across the street, I can make out the images on the cloth—casually dressed human beings seated cross-legged with their bodies aflame. The group is likely

4

explaining that these people are, in fact, not adherents of Falun Gong, and that the whole self-immolation event at Tiananmen Square was an elaborate hoax produced by the Communist Party's 610 Office to persuade the populace that Falun Gong is an extremely dangerous cult, which jeopardizes social stability. At the same time, this allows the government to justify the merciless detention, torture, and murder of Falun Gong practitioners as well as the harvesting of organs from their incarcerated bodies.

I take a deep breath and return my gaze to the busty woman on the massage parlour sign. Her sweet smile and bodacious curves make me feel better about the world. I pull out another smoke and turn it over in my hands before lighting it up. I'm no chain-smoker; I just hate to wait.

I stand up and, for a split second, think of heading home to see if Laura is in a better mood.

No. Obviously, we need some space. Better to walk up and down these sidewalks for a while. Bringing Laura will only ruin your night.

I take my own advice and weave through the bustling bodies until I feel an appropriate amount of time has passed.

When I re-enter Duck Son, the food is already on the front counter, the dishes neatly stacked in a large paper bag. The Lao Dan swipes my card and smiles.

I smile, too.

Kung Pao fuckin' chicken!

II

GEORGE'S HOUSE IS NEVER LOCKED, AND VISITORS ARE expected to enter of their own accord. Following custom, I stumble in and holler to make myself known.

Katie runs to the entrance with a grin. "Food!" she exclaims, grabbing the paper bag out of my hands. I bend down to remove my shoes but can still see her out of the corner of my eye, peaking and sniffing at our dinner. Katie is undeniably attractive—even tonight with her Sanrio tank top and shaved head.

Her hairstyle, or lack thereof, isn't born of any illness but, rather, is designed to help her through a brief stint of celibacy while she completes her yoga-teacher training. And, given her usual head of hair, shaving it is probably a wise decision if she wishes to keep the predators at bay and reduce temptation.

"Where's Laura?" she asks.

"At home," I answer. "She didn't feel up to coming out, tonight. She's exhausted and still has some stuff to do for that internship before she goes to bed."

"Oh," she says, looking a tad disappointed. "Well, come on in. George is in the other room. I'll go get us some plates."

I find George sprawled out on an old loveseat he'd acquired from a back alley some years ago. Above him is a poster of *The Last Supper*, altered so as to be led by Ronald McDonald, and, on the opposite wall, is a faithful rendering of *The Kiss* by Gustav Klimt. An open beer rests between his legs and, on the table in front of him, sits a short bong and a laptop. The room is already hazy with smoke and vibrating with the sound of cellos and violins.

"Steverino! Pop a squat," he says, patting the cushion next to him. "Have a beer. Take a hit. Katie and I are watching *City Lights*."

I grab a beer from the case beneath the table and sit down. Sure enough, Charlie Chaplin's *City Lights* is flashing across the screen. The Tramp, Chaplin's most memorable character, is looking uncomfortable as he politely receives the alcohol inadvertently being poured down his pants by a drunken millionaire.

George and I have recently been exploring silent films and, so far, he claims to like *City Lights* best. Although we never openly discuss it, I think we both feel that it's important to engage things with our friendship. Otherwise, our conversations might devolve into nothing more than gossip and the weather.

"You should've showed her *The Gold Rush* first," I

suggest, referring to another of Chaplin's films.

"Why?"

"The dancing of the 'Oceana Roll'," I explain. George laughs. We had both been in stitches when The Tramp had stuck forks into a couple of dinner rolls and danced them about on his tablecloth like two golden slippers.

Katie returns without dishware or cutlery. "I think we'd better fix our plates in the kitchen," she says. "The coffee table's too small. It's on the counter whenever you two are ready."

"Alright," says George. "No rush. Let's just chill. Come sit and watch for a bit. Let Steven have a hoot before he eats."

I put down my can and start to pack a bowl.

I'm hungry.

"No Kelly?" I ask.

George is unresponsive—lost in the dance of shadows being played out in front of him.

"I don't know where Kelly is," Katie finally answers as she plops herself down onto the floor and begins rocking side to side on her back, a foot clasped in each hand.

George glances at her. "What's going on?"

"Happy Baby Pose," she says. "Stretching my prostate."

George seems not to hear. "Hey, this part's hilarious," he laughs, pointing at the laptop. "Look!"

The Tramp and his affluent friend are out on the town and, by this point, extremely drunk. Their antics are hysterical, but Katie seems uninterested. Maybe, her mind, like mine, is on the food.

A massive hit enters my lungs. "Pause it," I squeak, blowing out a significant contribution to the surrounding haze. "Let's eat."

Without waiting for confirmation, I race into the kitchen and start scooping food onto a plate, taking plenty of everything except mapo tofu.

One by one, we return to squeeze onto the alley-couch where we eat elbow-to-elbow as we continue to watch *City Lights*. By the time I've finished my second helping, The Tramp is rubbing himself with a rabbit's foot—just about ready to enter the boxing ring.

I take an after-dinner toke and exhale it across the screen. "Hey, where are the fortune cookies?" I ask, passing the bong to Katie whose plate is already in the kitchen sink.

"Still in the paper bag," she replies, bringing the device to her lips. Beside her, George has his face so close to his meal that a strand of hair is dangling in his tofu.

Our "fortunes," I discover, are no longer in the bag but on the counter. There are four—one for each of us and one for Kelly. The cookies from Duck Son don't contain fortunes of the normal variety. Rather, they house the words of Confucius and other sayings from *The*

Analects. I come back with all four and toss them onto the table. Katie takes the one pointing at her and I, of course, grab the one aimed in my direction. George follows suit.

I snap my cookie in half and remove the note.

"Chaos, like a deluge, spreads across the kingdom."

That doesn't sound good.

"Can I have Kelly's, too?" I ask hopefully.

"No," says Katie, "that's Kelly's. It won't work for you. Oh, and make sure you eat the paper, too," she adds. "Otherwise, your fortune won't come true."

"Really?" says George. "Didn't you say the other day that you like to scan the sidewalks of Chinatown for fortunes people have thrown away? I sure hope you don't eat those."

Katie looks sheepish. "Not if I don't like the fortune . . ."

"And what's yours, today? Worth eating?" George teases.

She sits up straight, clears her throat, and reads, "When the year becomes cold . . . the pine and the cypress will be the last to lose their leaves."

"Hmm . . ."

"I'm the pine and cypress," she explains, popping the slip of paper into her mouth.

George laughs. "Mine says, 'The flowers of the aspen-plum flutter and turn'. Seems good enough . . .

What's yours say, Steven?"

I don't respond. My attention is fixed on Kelly's cookie—only a foot away, still sealed in plastic and full of potential. Ribbons of smoke hover propitiously above it.

"Earth to Steven," calls George.

With some effort, I pull my gaze away from the unopened cookie and back to the fortune in my hands.

"Chaos, like a deluge, spreads across the kingdom," I read.

III

ALMOST AS SOON AS I LEAVE GEORGE'S, IT BEGINS TO RAIN. I have no umbrella. I never do, much preferring to get soaked than lug something around with me in case of a downpour. My hooded sweater will have to be protection enough, although, on a mid-October night like this one, I wish I had a bit more. The grass and alcohol help, of course. It's past midnight, and I'm buzzing.

In fact, I had drank and smoked more than usual—in part because of the state of things between Laura and I but also because of my fortune. From dinner onwards, it had looped through my mind like an epicycle along a deferent, and I had found it difficult to engage in meaningful conversation with my hosts.

Chaos, like a deluge, spreads across the kingdom.

What the hell was that supposed to mean?!

I decide to make my way back to Duck Son to acquire another cookie—a second opinion.

The place is packed as usual for a weekend night, but, thankfully, I'm able to secure a seat at a table for two near the kitchen. I order a pitcher of beer and a basket of fries. The latter, Duck Son makes stupendously despite the fact that batonnet-cut, deep-fried potatoes aren't a dish of Chinese origin.

Laura wouldn't approve of my late-night snacking. She's studying to be nutritionist. And with her internship fast approaching, she's health nutty. Literally loco. Just thinking about it makes me want to order a second basket.

When my items finally arrive, I make quick work of them, eager to receive my fortune. I place the last couple of fries into my mouth and shove the table's contents aside. Soon enough, the Lao Dan notices and comes by with my bill and cookie.

I tear apart the wrapper and crack it open.

"The river sends forth no map."

Son of a bitch. That's not very helpful, now, is it?

LAURA is in bed when I get home. I try my best to keep quiet but accidently slip into the closet door while pulling off my shoes. The minor ruckus provokes shouting from the bedroom.

I don't respond.

She's probably sleep talking.

She does that sometimes. Nothing intelligible—just

half words and mixed-up phrases.

I go into the living room and find the couch and a patchwork quilt.

Ahh . . . the sweet comforts of home.

The shouting continues from the other room.

"Goodnight!" I yell back. "Fais de beaux rêves!"

IV

Footsteps. Rattling. A bang.

I rip off my headphones to listen more closely.

Laura isn't back already, is she? Impossible. She only left fifteen minutes ago. Maybe, it's just the kids doing ding dong ditch . . .

Distinct knocking.

Shit.

Adrenaline pumping, I scramble out of bed. Where are my pants? I scan the floor. Laura's things are everywhere in neat piles, ready to be packed away.

There they are.

A pair of sweats sits scrunched up at the foot of the bed. I throw them on, toss my laptop into the other room, and make haste towards the door—my mind frantically searching for an excuse to explain why it's locked.

More knocking.

I twist the deadbolt and swing the door open with a nervous smile.

"Steverino!"

16

"George?" I usually hate when he shows up un-announced, but, this time, I'm simply relieved that he isn't Laura. "Come on in. Make yourself at home," I say, still trying to catch my breath. "What brings you to this neck of the woods?"

"Came to bid Laura fare-thee-well," he says.

"Oh. She won't be back for a bit—maybe another hour. She went to meet a friend of hers for coffee before she leaves. Something to drink? Beer? Whiskey? Coffee?"

"Tea sounds good."

"That wasn't an option," I laugh. "Chai okay?"

"Perfect."

I put the kettle on and grab myself a beer from the fridge. Still not right from the night before, I know a little hair o' the dog will do me good. I crack open the can, chug some back, and feel the cold, carbonated goodness bubble down my esophagus. The relief is instant. I've heard of all kinds of hangover cures, but a little beer is usually all I ever need. Only in times of real suffering will I resort to the recipe of a childhood friend: one hoot, one extra strength liquid-gel, a dirty Caesar, and a good jerk.

The kettle pops, and I pour George his tea just as he likes it—in a glass mug with an unhealthy amount of cream and sugar. I give it a stir and bring it out to the living room where I find George on all fours, fidgeting with the new vaporizer I'd purchased at the insistence of Laura who was allegedly concerned over the state of my lungs.

"Here," I say, handing him the cup.

"Thanks, buddy."

"Not a problem."

"Well, what're ya sayin'? Should we watch something?"

"Sure," I reply. "Where are we at?"

He digs into his disheveled backpack and pulls out the list we'd compiled. "Umm . . . *The Wind* by Victor Sjöström . . . 1928."

"*The Wind*, is it? I dealt with quite the wind last night, you know? That walk home was pretty nuts. Had to stop at Duck Son." I'm about to bring up the matter of splitting the cost of the Chinese food but decide to wait for a more appropriate time. "Okay, you get the vape fired up; I'll get the movie going."

I grab my laptop, shove a prong into the headphone jack, and position the screen so George won't be able to see the shades of grey I had been watching before he arrived. After deleting the evidence, I quickly go to work searching for the Sjöström picture. Most movies from the silent era are easy to find, and *The Wind* is no exception.

I glance at George. He's sitting cross-legged on the floor, starring out the window as vapour spirals into the bag in front of him.

"Found it," I announce. "Looks like Lillian Gish is in it, too."

"Fuck, that chick frightens me. If her performance is as disturbing as it was in *Broken Blossoms*, I won't be able to sleep tonight."

"Nonsense. Just have some whisky before bed."

The vaporizer bag, unbeknownst to George, is about to burst. I pluck it off the machine and stick it to my lips. We have yet to watch a silent film sober.

"So, what'd you get up to this morning?" I ask.

"I went to see my grandma in the nursing home."

"Really? How was that?"

"Well, she consistently forgets I exist. Still remembers my mom, though. Kinda sad . . . But, you know, there's several people in that ward with Alzheimer's or whatever, and it's interesting . . . The environment's always the same and they repeat the same shit, so you can work on perfecting your interactions with them. I mean, sometimes, I try out variations when I'm bored. But you get to know what they like to talk about, what they like to hear, how they like to hear it, you know? So, by the end of each visit, I can usually put my grandma in a pretty good place."

Comments like this make me truly appreciate George's friendship.

One more little puff and I pass the bag. "I haven't done jack shit today. Pretty much just got outta bed before you got here."

Neither George nor I have jobs. We had spent the

summer months, along with Laura, working in cherry orchards. The venture wasn't quite as lucrative as any of us had hoped, but it had still provided us with a bit of cushion. Even so, at this point, I'm already counting my pennies and know that the sooner I find employment the better. I'm sure George is in no hurry. He only has himself to look after, and his rent is far cheaper than ours. At least with Laura going back to our hometown for her internship, we won't have to pay for two places at the same time. Still, she will have other living expenses, and her internship—unpaid as it is—means I'll be the sole provider until spring.

George sucks back the rest of the vapour and reattaches the bag. "Well, I'm pretty baked," he declares. "I'd already been at the bong before I got here."

"Then, shall we enter *The Wind*?" I ask.

"Not yet. We'd better have another bag before entering anything with Lillian Gish. You get 'er goin'. I gotta take a shit."

In his absence, I smoke a bag and drain my beer. I'm on my way to the fridge to get another when Laura suddenly storms into the apartment.

"Whoa! What's going on? Why are you back so early?"

"Who's here?"

"George."

"Why is he here? You went there last night. I fuckin'

leave tomorrow, Steven, and you don't even wanna spend time with me."

"Whoa! Slow down," I say, moving in to give her a pacifying hug. "He just showed up. He came to say goodbye. What's going on?"

"Nothing," she replies, pushing me away. "I just went halfway across the city for nothing, and my supposed boyfriend doesn't even want to spend time with me on the day before I leave."

"That's not true," I protest. "Besides, George'll be outta here soon enough. Come into the living room. We're just about to start a movie."

"I don't have time for that crap, Steven. I've gotta get ready for my internship. I leave tomorrow morning, in case you forgot."

"I figured you might have a little extra time since you're back so early. Besides, you're already all organized. You just gotta throw your stuff into a couple of suitcases, and you're good to go . . . Come sit for a bit, at least. He did come to see you off."

"Fuck," she says, marching into the living room.

I follow after her. "Wanna hoot?" I ask, hoping to reset her with marijuana.

"No."

"Come on. Just a little one. It'll make you feel better."

She doesn't respond. I start the vaporizer.

We sit without speaking to one another for some

time—the hum of the vaporizer fan and the crackling of the plastic bag as it fills with smoke the only mediators until George arrives to scatter the tension.

He enters the room, panting like a wild animal that's undergone some sort of tribulation.

"Wow! That was intense in there!" he gasps, placing his hands on his knees for support.

"Yeah, took you long enough. What happened? Get lost in the mirror?" I ask.

"Mirror?! Can't you see these beads of sweat, Steven? I pretty much just gave birth! Almost called for an epidural!"

Comments like this, too, make me cherish our friendship.

"Oh . . . Hi, Laura", he says, suddenly realizing she's present by the sound of her characteristic giggle—an adorable eruption reminiscent of thousands of tiny bubbles popping midair.

"Hi, George. How are you?"

"Better than a couple of minutes ago," he answers. "Came by to say goodbye. You're off tomorrow, are you?"

"Yep, bright and early."

"Well, we're gonna miss you. You'll be back for Christmas?"

"No, I don't think so. My family's all out there. So is Steven's, so he's gonna come spend the holidays with me."

"Yeah, well, I don't know my work situation, yet," I say.

"What're you talking about? You'll just tell whoever when you apply that you need those days off. We already booked the tickets."

"Yeah, I wouldn't worry too much," offers George. "I'm sure you'll be able to get it off, Steven."

"I still don't know why he just doesn't move there with me," Laura complains.

"You'll be busy," I argue. "Besides, I like it here. I left our city for a reason."

The truth is that I want some time to myself, some time away from Laura. Over the past few days, I've pretended to be sad along with her as she prepares for the move, but, in reality, I'm excited. Beyond excited. No Laura. The place to myself. Quietude. Freedom. I can hardy wait!

"Hey, did you get a costume yet?" asks George, changing the subject.

"No, I was thinking I'd figure that out tomorrow," I reply.

"Costume for what?" questions Laura.

"Halloween party," answers George. "It's at this guy Peter's. I don't think you two have met him . . . Interesting cat, though. Huge house, too. It's perfect. And he's already got it all decked out. I was there last week. It's gonna be wild. The theme's 'Fear and Loathing in

Wonderland'. We're definitely gonna have to get some acid or something. If you can swing it, you should try to come back, Laura. It's gonna be awesome."

"Why didn't you tell me you were going to a Halloween party, Steven?" Laura asks, her face scrunched up and ferocious.

"I didn't? Oh, I thought I did," I lie.

"No, you didn't, and you know damn well you didn't."

I look at her, my entire countenance pleading with her to drop the subject until we are alone. Thankfully, she does. "Well, that sounds cool," she says, turning back to George. "What're you gonna go as?"

"Raoul Duke."

"What's that?"

"Hunter S. Thompson—the guy who did the *Fear and Loathing* books."

"Oh. And you, Steven?" she asks, contorting her face once again as she turns towards me.

"Don't know yet."

"And, are you going to do acid, too, Steven?"

"Yep, if we can get it."

Her face scrunches up to the point I think it might collapse in on itself.

"Well, should we watch a bit of this movie?" I propose, trying to move the conversation away from the party.

24

Laura stands up. "You guys go ahead," she says. "I'm gonna go get my stuff together."

"Wanna hoot first," I ask in one final attempt to alter her headspace.

"No," she says, refusing to look at me as she walks away.

Although George wasn't able to see the looks she had given me, that final "no" makes Laura's mood explicit, and, as he comes to sit next to me on the couch, he raises his eyebrows as if to say, "Holy shit. What's with her?"

I simply shrug, fire up the vape, and hit play on the laptop.

The Wind acts as a great escape, and Lillian Gish, playing Letty Mason, is terrifically disturbing as expected—her frightened, shifty eyes certainly enough to warrant the nightcap I'd suggested earlier. We watch it straight through, journeying with Letty from Virginia to the ruthless Texan desert where she settles down, becomes miserably married, and is tormented day and night by sandstorms until, finally, she confronts the horse demon responsible for the perpetual tempest. In the final shot, she stands transformed, resting in her husband's arms, facing the wind in marital bliss.

Maybe, that's what my relationship needs—Laura to come face-to-face with a crazy horse spirit.

V

SEEING LAURA OFF IS HARDER THAN I'D EXPECTED. AS WE hug goodbye, she starts to cry, and her tears draw out my own. I think we both sense that her move will either give our relationship the time and space it needs or else be its final, destructive blow.

As difficult as it is, though, by the time I get home, my tears have dried, and I'm beginning to relish in my newfound separateness. I recognize immediately that the apartment is marked by a kind of tranquility that would be impossible with Laura cohabiting the place.

I pour a cup of water and go into the living room. As I sit down, I can't help but notice the many plants surrounding me: arrowhead vine, snake plant, dracaena, some lithops. That's one thing that Laura and I have in common—we both prefer living spaces filled with vegetation. And, as a result, our apartment is somewhat of a jungle.

Routine watering will be necessary. The other household duties can be shirked until I feel so motivated, but a drought is unacceptable. And, with Laura gone, the chore will me mine alone.

At the moment, my task is not to water plants, however, but to find a Halloween costume. I figure the internet is the best place to look. After all, retail outlets are forming ghost malls, aren't they? The masses must have shifted to online shopping for good reason.

I type "Alice in Wonderland costumes" into the search bar and get an eyeful of what an older generation might call indecency. Personally, though, I love role-play, love slutty costumes, and love Halloween for the excuse it gives to dress out of the ordinary. Unfortunately, Laura is pretty traditional when it comes to sex and pretty modest when it comes to dressing up. Don't get me wrong; we enjoy our time in the bedroom. But I'm an explorer. Laura . . . well, Laura is content.

I flit through various outfits and soon discover that online shopping guarantees consumers only two things—convenience and a great selection—not necessarily great prices. The costumes themselves aren't all that expensive but, given the date, I'm going to have to tack on expedited shipping.

Fuck that. I'll make an in-store purchase, thank you very much.

And so, I'm off to the local supercentre. That'll be my best bet. There are proper costume stores, of course, but my mother had always warned me against those. "Their

27

prices are through the roof."

Only three or four stops away, I could walk, but the damp, windy weather draws me to public transportation. From inside the bus, the world looks different—looks beautiful; the sun is shining, and rhythmic gusts are twirling about the autumn leaves.

I try to keep my attention fixed on the exterior display. Inside, there is little to be desired—just tightly packed, stinking, wet people, encased in advertisements that look as though they'd been coloured with high-lighter pens.

Not that I have much choice. The girl next to me is overweight and forcing me tight to the window. Apparently, she's stuck in some kind of loop that sees her repeatedly wrapping then unwrapping a donair, shoving a bit into her mouth, then wrapping it up again. She's trying to practice self-control, I imagine. But that donair looks and smells delicious. I don't know that I would've been able to put it away even once.

The bus stops directly in front of the supercentre. I climb over the girl and squeeze my way through the standing passengers until I'm sucked up into the flow of bodies pouring out onto the curb.

Fresh air. Freedom.

I enjoy a quick spliff and then walk towards the sales-giant as if to re-intern myself. It's spewing hot air like bad breath, and its automated doors are snapping like leviathan jaws.

I leap into the monster's mouth and down its cavernous throat.

Its insides are strange. Candy and Halloween decorations all over everything. It's as if the creature has eaten some sort of ghastly piñata.

I feel surprisingly good, though—oddly energized. The lights are bright, and the music is cheery. Now, to locate the costumes . . .

The place is massive, so, to save time, I ask a staff member for directions. "Follow me," she replies, with a flourish of her work smock. I would love to see her try on some of the outfits. But alas—the supercenter is no place for the suggestions of a lecherous goat. Reluctantly, I let her go with a quick "thanks" and carry on to ruffle through the costumes alone. I find three that are suitable: a "Mad Hatter", an "Alice", and a "Queen of Hearts". Thinking I won't be in the mood for cross-dressing on acid, I grab the former and make my way to the checkout. On route, I notice a recruitment sign near the costumer service counter. "JOIN THE TEAM!" it reads. "FULL OR PART TIME EMPLOYMENT OPPORTUNITIES! GREAT BENEFITS!"

I need a job, but the supercentre definitely isn't my first choice. Besides, I don't have a resume with me, and starting work before the party isn't an option. There's no way I am going to risk missing it for the sake of some shit job. Maybe, I'll come by again sometime after Halloween.

I purchase the costume and go to investigate further. Pay is above minimum wage. Flexible hours. That sounds not bad.

Fuck it. I'll just fill out the application and tell them I can't start until November. And, in the meantime, I'll apply at some other places, too.

I scribble in my info and hand it to the representative behind the counter.

"Just a minute," she says. "I'll go get the store manager."

I try to tell her that doing so is unnecessary, but she turns on her heel and is gone before I can say another word.

She returns a moment later with a man who is as tall as he is wide and looks as though he hasn't slept in days. "Hi, I'm Michael, the manager here," he explains in a voice both confident and subdued.

"Hi," I say, extending my hand. "I'm Steven."

"Nice to meet you, Mr. Steven. So, you're lookin' for some work, eh?"

"Correct."

"Great. I'm just in the middle of something, right now. But why don't you come back in like half an hour, and we'll do an interview, okay?"

Against my better judgement, I agree.

VI

HALF AN HOUR LATER, I'M BACK AT CUSTOMER SERVICE, asking for Michael.

"Come with me," says one of the girls behind the counter.

I follow her down a dank corridor filled with broken merchandise and flanked by windowed offices. She stops at a door near the end of the hall and knocks.

"Come on in," calls a voice.

The girl opens the door just enough to stick her head through. "Steven is here for his interview," she explains.

"Great. Thanks, Aadhya. Send him in."

She opens the door completely, revealing Michael's huge frame behind a paper- and binder-covered desk. The only light in the room is a buzzing florescence, and the walls are covered with cheesy, motivational posters. Any sensible individual would be forced to conclude that the workspace is undesirable. Yet, Michael seems oddly content.

"Hey, Steven. Come on in. Take a seat," he says,

motioning to one of the two uncomfortable-looking chairs in front of his desk. "Now, first things first—are you looking for part time or full time?"

I hesitate. I previously messed up an interview by answering this question wrong. Well, not so much wrong as strangely. Roberto's Pizza was hiring, and when Old Roberto asked me my preferred number of hours, I fumbled my words—went from full time to part time back to full time and then said a bunch of things that made it seem like I didn't know my sausage from my pepperoni. In the end, I ordered a slice of pizza and ate it in front of him. I can't remember if I tipped. I probably did. Either way, he never called, and my career in Italian cooking was over before it ever began.

"Umm . . . whatever you guys need," I reply.

"Well, we're only hiring part-time right now. Thirty-eight hours a week. Think you can handle that?"

"Yeah, that sounds fine."

"And are you able to work nights?"

Working the night shift sounds appealing. The store would be closed. I wouldn't have to deal with any customers.

"Yeah, nights aren't a problem."

"Then, for now, I think what we'll do is put you down for overnights, okay? There'll be an opportunity to move to days later on if you're interested. A lot of our staff switches back and forth . . . Now, Steven, what do you think are some of your strengths and weaknesses?"

"Umm . . . "

"I need at least one strength and one weakness."

"A strength . . . umm . . . I'm a team player. I'm punctual. Umm . . . "

"Good. And you've got a great smile. That's three. Now, how about a weakness?"

"Umm . . . "

"Well, I can tell you one. You get nervous real easy. Really happy then really nervous."

"Okay . . . "

"Okay. Good enough. I just need to fill out these damn interview reports they give me. I already looked over your application, and I see no reason why not to hire you. Congratulations! You got the job. You can start the day after tomorrow."

"Well, actually, I can't start until November second. I'd put that on my application."

"Oh, yes . . . I see that. In that case, be here on the second. Shift starts at ten."

VII

OCTOBER THIRTY-FIRST—HALLOWEEN AND QUITE POSS-
ibly my favorite night of the year. My costume doesn't fit
well. It's far too large, making me look more like
Chaplin's Tramp than the Mad Hatter. But I don't mind.
It's comfortable enough, and I feel as though I won't have
any trouble bringing a little extra madness to the outfit.

We're already a few drinks in, listening to "White
Rabbit" as we clunk our way to Peter's house in George's
rusted Grand Marquis. Katie is with us, too—dressed in
the pink and purple stripes of a Cheshire Cat. We have
yet to drop the acid. We all agreed that we had better
make it to the event first. One never knows where one
might decide to go once a psychedelic has been ingested.
Or whether or not the site of administration will be left
at all.

George parks the car a few houses down from
Peter's and flicks on the interior light.

"You got the scissors, Steven?"

"Sure do," I answer, reaching into my pocket. I pull

out a pair of cuticle scissors and hand them to George who immediately goes to work cutting up our Scooby-Doo blotter paper.

"Alright. Four for you . . . and four for you," George says, handing Katie and I our respective doses. "We a' gonna be flyin'!"

"Cheers," says Katie.

The three of us "clink" our bits of paper before popping them into our mouths for what I know is going to be a long, anxious chew.

I step out of the car and look back at Katie and George. Katie is still scrambling out of the vehicle, and George is waving his arms around like Raoul Duke.

"Holy Jesus! What are these goddamn animals?" he shouts.

I chuckle. "Let's get in there."

PETER'S house is large and fantastically decorated with a wide array of *Fear and Loathing* and *Alice in Wonderland* paraphernalia—half-painted flowers, giant chess pieces, a replica of the Las Vegas sign. One room has been transformed into a poker den; another, a hookah lounge; a third, a tearoom. They have croquet out back, and the main room, which all guests enter upon, has been gutted of furniture so as to provide space for a dancefloor.

As we walk in, two women, both resembling Alice, are spinning circles around a man dressed like the Ace of Spades. Not everyone, however, is in appropriate attire. There's a Santa outfit, and one figure on the floor looks as though it's wearing a Darth Vader costume gone wrong.

"Hey, Kelly's here!" Katie yells, running towards the monstrosity.

"Come on," says George, pushing me forward. "I'll introduce you to Peter."

We eventually find our host in the tearoom, sipping whisky from a teacup. He is fatter than I'd expected, balding, and has beady eyes. His costume is that of a pig clad in infant's dress.

George leaps in front of him, and the two embrace. "Steven, this is Peter," he tells me once they're no longer pressed up against one another. "Peter, this is Steven."

"Hi, Steve. How da ya do?" says Peter at high-speed, grinning as he speaks. "Welcome to 'Fear and Loathing in Wonderland'! Happy to have you here. Come. Sit. What da ya guys drink? Whisky?"

"Whisky sounds fan-tastic," George answers.

Peter continues speaking as he pours the drinks, his pace unaltered. "I was an investor before," he rambles. "Now, an artist. Actually, got a big show coming up on New Years Eve. You boys oughta come. I was miserable

36

before. Everyone around me was miserable. All miserable cunts. Family. Friends. Colleagues ... "

An Alice walks in and takes a seat at the table. The acid is already starting to kick in. I smile at her—teeth and eyes. She smiles back.

" ... Hey, you boys wanna snoot?" asks Peter. "Freud thought coke was so great that he gave his fiancé a palm-sized rock of the stuff for a pre-wedding present."

"I'm okay," I reply. "We actually took four hits of acid earlier."

"Up, down, or all around—suit yourself."

"Hey, I actually gotta take a leak. Where's the nearest washroom?"

"Just down the hall, brother."

I'm feeling nauseous and need a little timeout from the party. The washroom is a perfect sanctuary—cold, brightly lit, undecorated, and relatively quiet. I take off my clothes and lay down like the figure in da Vinci's *Vitruvian Man*, my feet an inch from the door. This acts as an added safety. The doorknob lock is confusing, and I can't be sure I've locked it properly.

Just stare at the ceiling and breathe. Don't close your eyes. Stay away from the mirror. Breathe ...

I stay steady for some time, but then unfamiliar and ferocious sounds begin growing out of the music. They are entering my refuge, turning my stomach.

Holy shit ... I gotta throw up.

I roll over. Saliva floods my mouth, and demons scream up my esophagus.

Wait. Where do people puke? Sink or toilet?

I choose the sink. Chunks of potato and whole macaroni noodles fill the basin, and I'm forced to run the tap and mash the pieces down with my bare hands.

Banging at the door.

Fuck. How long have I been in here?

"Coming," I yell, grabbing my costume and rushing to make myself presentable. A shower would be nice.

I can't believe I puked. I usually only puke on mushrooms.

I glance at the mirror and grin at the Mad Hatter staring back at me. "Get in there, Steven. Back to the tea party!"

I pull open the door and step into the hall. The walls are already breathing, and the floor is covered with Escherian lizards.

Now, where's that tearoom? Left! Left! Left!

Fuck, who builds a hall like a funnel to a rabbit snare?

Three lefts make a right.

Bingo!

The tearoom is absolute madness—sentient beings everywhere—Tweedledees, Tweedledums, a flamingo—and none of them drinking tea.

No available seats either.

My world starts spinning—not in the simple way

that it does for a drunkard but, rather, in multiple directions—no, in multiple dimensions, simultaneously.

"He took me for his housemaid."

"It was Bill, I fancy."

The voices come to me from various conversations, all at once, and entirely comprehensible.

" . . . That girl understood. She fell in love with me."

"You're a serpent; and there's no use denying it."

" . . . some kind of electric snake."

"Go round and get it at the window."

"Bill's got the other."

"One toke? You poor fool!"

"You shouldn't have put it in with the bread-knife."

"Order some golf shoes."

"There's no use crying like that!"

"You okay?"

"I suppose I ought to eat."

"It won't stop. It's not *ever* going to stop."

Something grabs my arm.

"Steven!"

VIII

"STEVEN! YOU OKAY?! YOU DON'T LOOK SO GOOD." IT'S A she-rabbit.

"Huh? . . . Yeah—just a little dizzy."

"Come on. Let's go somewhere quiet and get you some water."

"Just trippin' a bit."

"I know. George told me. Come on. You look like you need something to drink."

What I need is to get my dance on, get a good sweat going, feel the beat.

"Come on," she insists, pulling my arm.

"My apologies, Miss Rabbit," I say. "But the dancefloor's a callin'!"

KELLY is still dancing—so is the Ace of Spades. I pounce onto the floor somewhere between them and begin shuffling my legs. It starts off slow . . . One foot.

Two foot. Three foot. Hop. Then, suddenly, the music pierces me. I become impregnated with its spirit. My eyes shut of their own accord. My dance quickens—escalates into a four-limbed frenzy. I feel novel, connected, beautiful.

When finally I open my eyes, a Queen of Hearts is dancing towards me. The acid can see past her makeup, but she's still attractive. Moves well, too. With feet still tapping, I bow my torso. She smiles, curtsies, and our respective dances begin to form a harmony.

Being psychoactively enhanced, however, my endurance far outmatches hers. After only a few songs, she visibly weakens. Seeing she needs a break, I take hold of her hand and lead her to a sofa in the adjacent room, where we both melt into its leather.

I had no doubt been giving her suggestive glances as we danced, but it still comes as a surprise when she abruptly straddles me and pushes her tongue past my lips. It feels strange, her tongue—feels like some bizarre, alien object has entered my mouth—something stiff and dense like a silicone spatula. I try to be polite and accept the kiss for as long as I can bare, but, in the end, I'm forced to gently push her away.

"Sorry," I squeak. "I'm trippin' balls. I can't do this right now."

She unsaddles herself, and I let my head fall back onto the couch.

I close my eyes.

Before me is a slowly rotating, gold and red kaleidoscope. I've seen it before, and I know what to do. I begin rocketing up towards its center. As I pick up speed, a familiar giggling erupts, briefly enveloping me before I break through to the other side.

But once past the threshold, everything is different. Unfamiliar. Cold and silent. There is a lake, but it's motionless. There are waves, but they're still. There are fish, but they seem frozen in time with their bodies sticking halfway out of the water.

Then, there are stars and a row of tiny, floating creatures like gremlins, each grasping a flip-clock wheel.

What are these . . .

We're horopalettologists. We're here to unveil to you your time of death.

No. No thanks. I don't wanna to see it.

But, despite my objection, their wheel leaves start flipping at high speeds. I try to look away, but the horopalettologists are in control. I can't. The best I can do is will myself not to read the digits on the leaves as wheel after wheel comes to a halt. Year. Month. Day. Hour. Minute. Second. Millisecond . . . Like an endless matryoshka doll, the little, wheel-bearing creatures shrink into the horizon.

My eyes shoot open.

Where the fuck is George? I gotta get outta here!

IX

WHEN I FIND HIM, GEORGE IS IN THE HOOKAH DEN, blowing smoke rings with a caterpillar.

"Steverino! How's that acid treating you?"

"Strong," I say, taking a seat next to him.

"Here, have some tequila. It's crazy. It just dissipates into nothingness. No buzz, no burn—just the sweet taste of blue agave."

I take the bottle and have a swig. George is right.

"So, what've you been up to?" he asks.

"Dancing."

"Right, I saw you on the floor with that Queen of Hearts."

"Yeah, I shouldn't of done that."

"There's nothing wrong with a little dancing, Steven."

"Yeah, but then we kissed."

"And then?"

"I don't know. I didn't really kiss her back."

"Then, no harm, no foul!"

"I guess so. Let's just hope no one saw, and it doesn't get back to Laura."

"Man, I wouldn't worry too much about it. Just enjoy the night. You know what I try to do before a party, though? Jerk it before coming. A tug or two makes me deaf to sirens."

"You're sick."

"Here, have some hookah."

"No. I think I need some fresh air. I'm gonna go for a stroll. If we can't find each other later on, let's just meet back at your place, okay?"

"Okay, Steverino. Enjoy!"

MY exit is swift. And I have no intention of returning. I've had enough costumed chaos for one night. My flight, however, lands me in suburbia—a cold and lonely place to be in any season, never mind at the end of October on a psychedelic drug.

Maybe I should just hangout in George's car.

No. I'll walk. It's not that far. An hour. Maybe two.

Wait a tick . . .

A small group of reptiles approaches a minivan.

"Hey, are you guys headin' back?" I yell.

"Unfortunately," answers the nearest one. "These two dipshits gotta work in the morning."

"Mind if I catch a ride?"

"Where are you goin'?" asks another, fumbling keys—clearly the driver.

"I live near Chinatown. But anywhere in and around downtown is fine."

"Well, we're all Little Portugal."

"Yeah, that's cool. I can walk from there."

"Alright. Hop in, brother."

THE drive is a blur—roughhousing in the backseat and twenty questions I can't answer. Nevertheless, when the reptiles drop me off and go on their merry way, we submit our goodbyes with a kind of substance normally reserved for true friends. Perhaps, they're tripping, too.

When I get to George's, I let myself in without the customary holler. Blacklights are on in the basement, which means Kelly is probably home, but shouting so late is inappropriate.

I pour a glass of water and make myself comfortable on the alley-couch. My body feels amazing. The peak of the trip is over. The walls are no longer breathing, and everything has ceased to be overlain with geometric patterns. The figures in the *The Kiss* and *The Last Supper* aren't exactly stationary, but they aren't morphing into golden dragons or twelve-limbed arthropods either.

I move into a horizontal position and begin reflecting on the evening and all that transpired. No matter which way I go, though, my mind keeps coming back to that leather sofa and the Queen of Hearts. In hindsight, I wish I had explored things further, had taken her to some other room where eyes couldn't reach us and our actions wouldn't leak back to Laura.

I love Laura and dread hurting her in any way. But, at the same time, I am desperate to explore another woman. I've been with Laura for thirteen years. And I was a virgin prior. Perhaps, I should've acted—should've finally ripped the monkey off my back. How am I supposed to go on for a lifetime like this? Surely, to know just one woman is to not know women at all . . .

I can picture the Queen of Hearts perfectly—her soft, white skin radiating like moonlight; her long, luscious lashes brushing her cheekbones as she blinks; the intoxicating smell of her gardenia-infused perfume; and the tickle of her hair as she hovers above my face and straddles my crotch.

A hand breaches my trousers.

What about Kelly?

It doesn't matter. I'm a master of discretion. Full steam ahead!

X

MY FIRST FEW DAYS OF WORK ARE TOLERABLE. PLENTY OF caffeine and the novelty of the tasks and environment make the time pass quickly. It's when a job becomes monotonous and the faces around one become too familiar that one begins to dread one's time on duty. Shift changes become as lifeless as those in Fritz Lang's *Metropolis* and individuals start yelling things, like "Father! Father! Will eight hours ever end??!!"

I'm primarily responsible for restocking shelves. And, as Michael (the manager) is quick to point out, this isn't difficult. "Place new stock behind the old, English labels out. That's it. Ain't rocket science," he says.

Two employees are assigned to each aisle. I'm paired up with a scrubby looking fellow by the name of Omari. We don't converse much since we start each shift at opposite ends of the aisle and work towards one another. It's only after several hours of steady stocking that we finally come close enough to speak to each other at a comfortable volume. Of course, by this point, I'm normally exhausted, and the last thing I want to do is open my mouth and wiggle my tongue.

Omari inevitably sparks up a conversation, though. Thankfully, it's more or less one-way. I just have to nod and grunt, and he goes on talking about his family, financial problems, the union. I honestly don't know where he finds the energy. He doesn't seem the type to powder his nose . . .

Aside from this last hour, stalking shelves provides me with an unhealthy amount of time to think. Very rarely, of course, do I consider the objects in front of me. Boxes of cereal and peanut butter jars are uninteresting. Sure, one can contemplate their means of production—the ingenuity of humans, their labour, and the natural conditions necessary for things like wheat and peanuts to grow. One can even meditate on weather patterns and the formation of celestial bodies. In fact, a person can follow cereal grains and legumes all the way back to the Big Bang, if they'd like. But this journey is fun only once or twice.

Not surprising, my neural pathways are, instead, becoming worn around much more captivating subject matter—the Queen of Hearts and the possibility of exploring foreign waters. The Queen is gone, of course. That ship has sailed. Besides, a voyage of that nature runs the risk of becoming common knowledge. I've heard of some couples swinging, being "open," or even forming sophisticated, polyamorous relationships. But while I am, perhaps, comparable to a man like Jacques Cartier, Laura can be compared to no sailor at all. Never will she dream of constructing a massive haul or erecting a sail in search of something extraordinary. She takes to water, instead, like a swan—content to let the waves move her aimlessly about so long as her lifelong partner floats alongside her.

Despite Laura's tendencies, however, I cannot help my own. By workday two, my cargo is loaded, and, by workday three, I have the bowsprit wholly aimed at distant shores. Laura's internship provides me with the perfect opportunity to up-anchor. I have to be stealthy, however. Even George can't know. And, for similar reasons, it's preferable if the girl's English is nonexistent.

By workday four, I've ascended to the crow's nest and honed in on the massage parlour above Duck Son.

By workday five, my ship is under full sail.

XI

ADMITTEDLY, I'M NERVOUS, EVEN AFRAID TO SATIATE MY curiosity. My fear isn't identifiable with the kind found in nature, though—in the hearts of barnacle goslings, for instance, when they first take flight. It is, rather, distinctly human, a fear born of moral uncertainty. Yet, if Laura and I are to last, a trip to the massage parlour is necessary. I just hope a simple rub n' tug will be sufficient.

To gather strength and to create a temporal buffer between my apartment and the massage parlour, I undertake a solitary pub-crawl. I think part of me believes that, if I create enough time and space between walking out my door and climbing those greasy steps above Duck Son, I'll feel as though my actions aren't premeditated.

I have two or three bars in mind, but, in the end, I visit four. The first is a somewhat grungy joint called Pistons. George and I have been before. It's nothing special, but it has an antique jukebox and a beer-stained pool table that doesn't cost any money. No TVs or VLTs, either, which I appreciate. Such devices are a sure way to ruin a venue's lighting.

I order a pint and make myself comfortable at a lonely table near the pool cues. I had hoped to drink alone, but, after only a few sips, a slim, craggy man approaches my table, grasping what appears to be a Red Needle. He helps himself to the seat opposite mine and launches a barrage of statements, stories, and questions. I listen politely, nodding as he speaks, providing responses when necessary.

"Would you eat a live-caught fish?"

"I don't see why I wouldn't," I answer. "Would you?"

"Well, yes, I used to eat them all the time."

I start drinking faster.

"Do you know why I come to Pistons, young man?"

"I don't know. Why?"

"For the table. I like breaking the balls, seeing them scatter. Fat butterflies. Lots of colours—like the ones at my father's grave."

"I see."

"He died when I was just seven, and my mother used to make me clean the bird droppings off his tombstone because I was the youngest . . . "

Fan blades are spinning in the reflection of my glass. *One more sip . . .*

"Shall we have ourselves a game?"

I chug back the rest of my beer. "No, I've actually gotta get goin'. I'm on my way to meet someone. Nice talking with you, though."

"Nice talking with you, too, Steven."

Steven? Had I mentioned my name?

THE second and third bars are located side by side. The former is an extremely narrow place stuffed with old furniture and abstract paintings. If not for the shelves of alcohol, one might mistake it for nothing more than a fancy hallway. The other plays songs like "Desert Rose" and "Ring of Fire" and boasts an impressive collection of arcade machines. I drink a gin martini at the first, a beer at the second.

My fourth stop isn't exactly a bar. It's, rather, the lounge of a KTV. I'm only about a block from Duck Son when, suddenly, I feel the need for a little extra courage. So, I enter the nearest karaoke place and order myself a whisky and green tea.

The lounge is staffed by elegantly dressed Chinese and has the atmosphere of an English palace overloaded with neon lights. The guests, though, are young and not nearly as refined as their expensive clothes and environment suggests. Most are more concerned with their cellphones than engaging their company. And a trip to the washroom reveals toilets full of shit and urinals peppered with cigarette butts.

That said, they are a friendly bunch. And when, after my third or fourth drink, I approach a group of them, they welcome me with hoots and hollers. I join in their game of Liar's Dice and, after a few rounds, am, perhaps, unduly open and comfortable. I ask a few of them about the massage parlour above Duck Son. They claim to have never been themselves but assure me that it does have a reputation for providing services above and beyond the call of duty. I ask about prices. They aren't sure.

I have a few more goes with the dice but lose every turn. My glass empty, the group insists I order another, that I seek redemption—but I think I'd better not try. Luck isn't with me. And, if my plan is to succeed, I can't have too many whiskies.

I stand up and go to pay for my drinks, peaking inside my wallet as I wobble over. My cash is dwindling.

Damnit. I'm gonna have to put it on the card.

Ideally, I don't want a record of any of the night's events. But, if there is to be evidence of something, I prefer it be of my time at the KTV over the massage parlour.

The girl at the till hands me a card reader. It asks for a tip.

Goddamnit. Tip after tip after tip. All of these bar-tenders feeling entitled for having done little more than poured a drink. Tipping culture can rot in hell. Post the price with wages considered. Don't make drunks do math!

I punch in a number and hand the card reader back to her.

Fuck, tonight's gonna cost me.

XII

I SLIP SPRINTING UP THE STAIRS TO THE MASSAGE PARLOUR.
I figure the quicker I am the less likely I'll be seen. But
the steps are as greasy as those to Duck Son. My right
knee goes down hard, and my face smacks the railing.

A groan escapes my throat and echoes off the
surrounding storefronts.

*Get yourself together, Steven! You got work to do.
Stop slippin' and slidin' on deck and man the goddamn
sails!*

I brush myself off and enter the parlour through its
frosted glass doors. The interior is tranquil. Like many
such establishments, the space is infused with the sound
of trickling water and the smell of reed diffusers; soft
light passes through paper lampshades and images of
blue and white lotuses cover the walls.

I exchange nervous grins with the matron behind
the counter.

"Hello," she calls. "Massagy?"

"Yeah, umm—"

"Oh! You bleedin'!" I touch my face where it had been injured. There isn't much blood, but there is some. "Xiao Li!" screams the matron. A young woman appears out of nowhere and begins administering a bandage.

"I slipped on the stairs," I explain as the girl finishes up, but the comment doesn't register with either of them.

My wound looked after, the old lady returns to business. "What one you want?" she asks, pointing to a laminated list of services. I stare at it for a while, but the alcohol in my system is making the words stutter. I turn to the prices. Numbers. I can still do numbers.

"That one," I say, pointing to the most expensive service. Surely, such a pricy package will include all that I've come for.

"Okay," she smiles. "You go there. Shower."

I go to the room she indicates. A young man inside shows me to my locker and helps me stow away my things. I strip naked, put on the rubber sandals he offers, and hop into the shower.

The water is scalding. I yelp and jump out of the stream.

"Everything okay?"

"Fine," I lie, shutting off the tap. "Water's a bit hot, that's all."

"It should get better," he says. "Give it a minute."

I readjust the showerhead so that it's aimed at one of the tiled walls and fire. Steam rises ferociously and floods over the curtain.

Well, this ain't happening.

I squat in a safe place, take several deep breaths, and pee.

Five minutes later, my position hasn't changed, so I turn off the water and step back out into the changing room.

"Here you are, sir," says the young man, handing me a towel. "You're to wear the clothes laid out on the bench. Take your time."

I dry off and throw on the outfit—thin pajama shorts and a matching shirt.

All the mirrors are fogged over. I walk over to one and clear away a circle of condensation. My hair is a mess. I comb a hand through it and rip the drooping bandage from my face. Even though this isn't a romantic affair, for some reason, I still want to look presentable.

"If you're ready, sir, please follow me."

He brings me into a dark room and suggests I make myself comfortable on one of its massage tables.

"Your masseuse will be with you shortly," he informs me, shutting the door behind him.

I remove my shirt and climb onto the table. But, as I lay down, something activates my adrenal glands. Flight or fight or . . .

I shove my face into the little hole.

That feels better.

I've just about got my heartrate back under control when a light knock at the door sends it into overdrive.

"Hello ... massagy ... "

My masseuse has arrived.

I lift my head to peek at her but can't make out her face in the darkness. Perhaps, this is best, though. This way, we'll be unable to recognize one another if ever we have a chance encounter.

She douses my back with oil and climbs onto the table. I had been expecting her to massage with her hands, but she performs, instead, with her feet. Aside from the odd cough and slip of a heel, the experience is a pleasant one. The alcohol helps, I suppose. Normally, I'm a ticklish mess on a massage table. I discover, however, that, after a few drinks, I am much more submissive.

Some time passes this way, and I'm beginning to wonder whether or not I'll be receiving additional services when, suddenly, the masseuse removes my shorts and begins running her feet across my anus in subtle, rhythmic swoops. This is the first time anyone has ever touched this surprisingly sensitive part of my body, and I desperately want her to continue.

Give me an hour of this!

But, before I can vocalize my request, she jumps off the table. Landing with a thud, she spits out the lozenge she'd been sucking, turns me over, and begins servicing me at high-speed with her mouth.

What the fuck?!

I pull back, but she seems oblivious to my discomfort. And, with a giggle, she climbs back onto the
table and lays face up—her robe already removed.

"Come on me," she beckons in thickly accented
English.

I take her to mean "cum," so I move in between her
legs and begin stroking myself. To my surprise, I can feel
and smell latex.

When'd she wrap me up?!

I don't have much time to consider the question,
though, for, a moment later, she grabs ahold of me, and,
without warning, unites our genitals.

AFTERWARDS, I desperately want to shower, but the
water, still too hot, forces me to settle for a bird bath
instead.

When I get out of the changing room, the matron is
still standing behind the counter. She looks older than
before. So does the wallpaper. Without making eye
contact, I hand her the cash from my wallet and walk
away.

I am about to leave when I turn impulsively to the
little shrine near the exit. I can't tell if the central deity is
Guan Yu or Baimei Shen, but I bow three times

regardless. "Please, bless me, God," I beg with each humbling gesture.

When I get to the bottom of the stairs, a group of girls are snickering at something in front of Duck Son. A few of them look at me, and their laughter seems to intensify.

I fix my eyes to the sidewalk as I brush past them.

Home, Steven. Just get home.

XIII

WHAT'D THAT BITCH DO TO ME?!

My meatus has a pulse and my shaft feels like it's been slammed in a door.

Must have been that aggressive fellatio . . .

I roll out of bed and go straight to the medicine cabinet above the bathroom sink, grab the bottle of ibuprofen and pop two—one for each of my headaches.

The medicine cabinet is a mess. So is the rest of the room. Urine is pooled on the floor, specks of vomit cover the toilet, pill bottles are in the sink, and my toothbrush is partway down the bathtub drain. The night before, I had brought it into the shower with me in a mad attempt to clean myself thoroughly. I recall several soap-and-rinse cycles, teeth brushing, mouthwash gargling, cutting, shaving, and, in the end, prostrating myself with ass held high.

I turn my back on the mess, go into the kitchen, and put on a cup of coffee. Cleaning the washroom will have to wait until I can stomach it.

As my coffee brews, I lean against the counter and consider the pictures on our fridge door. Laura had stuck them there with magnets. The collection started with a strip from a photo booth but has since grown into quite a display. At the center of it all is a picture of the two of us celebrating our five-year anniversary at an all-inclusive in Mexico's Yucatán Peninsula. In the image, my face is severely sunburned. Laura's is nicely bronzed. We had just returned from Chichen Itza where Laura had repeatedly applied sunscreen and encouraged me to do the same. I had ignored the advice. In fact, I distinctly remember climbing the three hundred sixty-five steps to the summit of Kukulcan's temple and laughing at the sun while I waited for Laura to reach the top. That night, when we got back to the resort, she applied aloe vera to my face with more than one I-told-you-so.

I rip the picture off the fridge, flip it over, and angrily place a round, black magnet on its backside as if making the first move in a game of Hex. Wishful thinking, I suppose.

BY evening, my hangover has disappeared, but the penile pain persists. It's there the following afternoon when I awake, and on the third and fourth days as well.

My work suffers. It isn't important work, of course.

I'm not performing surgery or practicing statecraft or anything of that nature. Nevertheless, I'm moving at about three-quarters-speed and forcing Omari to pick up my slack.

When I groan and moan to wakefulness on the fifth day, the first thing I do is make two phone calls. One is to Laura to tell her that I am well and that I love her. The other is to the supercentre to let them know I won't be coming in that evening. I have a fever. Urination hurts. Erections are painful. Normally, I don't like adding additional stress to our already overburdened healthcare system, but it's time to see a doctor.

Never one for regular checkups, I have no family physician. As a result, I find myself at a walk-in clinic owned and operated by a surprisingly youthful doctor by the name of Vincent Garrett. The usual procedure ensues: check in, two hours of waiting with nothing but crap magazines to read, admittance into a private room, more waiting, and then, finally, the physician's grand entrance.

Doctor Garrett doesn't seem too concerned about my condition. "No puss or anything. Probably just a minor infection," he explains. "I'll write you up a prescription for a bit of antibiotics and some phenazopyridine. You should be feeling better in a few days. Make sure to finish your pills regardless."

"Will do," I say.

"We'll send you to the lab to do some blood and urine tests, too, which you should try to get done sometime today. If you wait, the antibiotics might mask what's going on in there. Oh, and refrain from any sexual activities until everything clears."

I fill my prescription and go straight to the lab. And, almost the moment after my blood is drawn and urine collected, I take my first round of antibiotics and phenazopyridine. There is no way in hell I am going to mess with a doctor's instructions when it comes to my precious pearls.

For the rest of the day, I desperately try to relax, to heal—but I can't. I'm nervous, restless. I'll lay down for a moment and then abruptly get up, check about a dozen medical websites, and spend an even greater chunk of time staring at my genitals. I attempt to watch *Le Voyage dans la Lune* but can't bear the sight of a functioning rocket.

How the hell did I get an infection anyway?! Wasn't I wearing a condom? Jesus, I just wanted a handjob...

I take out my medicine and pour a glass of water.

And what about Laura? What if I don't get better before I'm supposed to see her at Christmas?

I pop the pills into my mouth and swallow.

Fuck, I'm itchy, too. What if I got crabs? Herpes?

What if I got HIV?!

THE following evening, I head to work. Although stocking shelves is miserable, I find the sight of Omari down the aisle and the occasional appearance of Michael somewhat comforting.

I'm even more unproductive than before. Yet, it beats being in our apartment. Of course, my ailment is still my mind's sole concern, but at least I'm not constantly on medical websites, looking at pictures of nasty urinary tract infections, and rolling about in psychological turmoil.

But I can't hide in the supercenter aisles forever.

When my eight hours are up, I return home.

Back in the apartment, my torment continues. Despite being exhausted, I find myself unable to sleep. Not only does my condition prevent me from laying on my stomach, to which I am accustomed, but floods of stress and worry are making my body tense up in strange ways. I suddenly notice my abdomen and thighs are tight. A foot cramps. I consciously try to relax it, but it refuses to obey. Even worse, attempts to calm my mind as a whole bring onslaughts of demonic content horrifying enough to make Boschian hells seem fluffy.

Eventually, I stop trying to sleep and go to the kitchen. The floor is cold and the room reeks of tuna. Several cans are soaking in the sink.

I open the fridge and stare at its contents—a half loaf of bread, a jar of pickles, mustard, some old apples, a beer. Alcohol might help, but I've placed it off limits along with grass and cigarettes. I remove a slice a bread from its bag, squish it into a little ball, and shove it inside my mouth.

Maybe, I should go to George's. They're probably all up and eating breakfast. We could watch a silent film. We could . . . No, I can't deal with that positive energy right now. Better to be alone. Gotta focus on healing . . .

I leave the kitchen and go into the living room to lay on the couch. The sun is up, its rays already slipping though the blinds onto the room's dehydrated plants and dusty furniture. I curl into the fetal position and pull a quilt over my huddled form. Traffic is in full swing—a steady hum of engines accented occasionally by a honk or a screech and rising ever so often into car-alarm crescendos.

I choose one of the plants, a viper's bowstring hemp, and vow to stare at it relentlessly until I fall asleep. The last thing I see before slipping from consciousness is a small spider descending down a dragline from one of its leaves.

XIV

A NUMBER OF DAYS HAVE PASSED SINCE I'VE SEEN DOCTOR
Garrett. Things seem stable—perhaps, even better,
although it's difficult to be sure. Maybe, I've just grown
accustomed to the pain. It certainly persists. But I trust in
the pills and figure I'll just check in again once the
prescription finishes. In the meantime, I'm determined to
supplement the medicine as much as I can with natural
remedies. Based on online advice, I start drinking
copious amounts cranberry juice, taking odorless garlic,
and rubbing myself with coconut oil. The internet also
appears to be full of individuals raving about the benefits
of particular poses and the power of Ayurveda, so I
decide I'll try yoga as well.

I contact Katie and explain that I'm not interested in
anything arduous. She suggests that we go together to a
yin yoga class. The name sound peculiar, but I agree.

We meet at her place. She's already standing outside
when I arrive, shouldering a yoga mat and clutching a
duffle bag in her mittened hands. I ask if George will be

joining us.

"Naw, he's trippin'," she says. "He ran out about an hour ago all excited. He claimed to have seen something called a tesseract."

"Where was he headed?"

"Didn't say," she replies, turning down the sidewalk.

I had hoped we'd take the bus, but Katie insists on walking. At least the weather isn't bad. The tight underwear I'd chosen were helping, too, by reducing the number of uncomfortable interactions with my pants.

"I don't think we've seen each other since the Halloween party," Katie starts. "What'd you think? Pretty wild, eh?"

"Yeah, crazy," I agree.

"You left kinda early, though."

"I guess so. I dunno know. Earlier than you and George anyway."

"So you met Peter Penguin?"

"Penguin? That's his last name?"

"No, its Cote. He just looks like the Penguin."

"The Penguin?"

"From Batman."

"Really?"

"Come on! I mean, if someone said like, 'Katie, you've got a week to make a Batman film with Penguin as the villain', I'd run to Peter. Recasting Danny DeVito would be my first choice, obviously, but I imagine he's a hard man to find."

I laugh. "Well, it was difficult to see the resemblance past the pig nose and giant baby clothes," I say.

Just being with Katie, I am already beginning to feel better.

"He's not doing too hot, though . . . "

"What?"

"Stage three cancer," she says. "You should really come to his art show in January. He says it's gonna be his last."

This information should send my mood spiraling back down. But, instead, hearing of Peter's suffering brings me comfort. Just knowing that other people—real people that I'd met and touched—were facing health issues brings me a sliver out of isolation.

As I march down the sidewalk after Katie, I can't help but feel my steps growing lighter.

NOT surprisingly, the studio's waiting room is primarily decorated with an eclectic mix of things Indian, Tibetan, and Japanese. Most striking in the space, however, is a series of elevated posters, all of which depict the same woman in various, unflattering poses. She's entirely naked in each and, in many, contorted so that she might stare at parts of herself that no human being should be able to see without technological aid.

69

The room also boasts complementary tea, which a number of yogis and yoginis are dispensing into tiny, handless, white cups and gently sipping. Katie pours me one. It's lukewarm and smells of jasmine.

I finish my portion in a single gulp and suggest we go into the studio and find ourselves some mats. Katie encourages me to go ahead. She has something she needs to ask the instructor.

I go in and lay supine on a mat near the back—the crown of my head aimed at the room's mirror in co-ordination with the other practitioners. The studio is dark but warm and comforting—something like an overly spacious womb. I can faintly hear those around me breathing. And the feeling of so many bodies gathered together in silence is sublime.

The tea drinkers slowly file in, the teacher at their rear. I twist my neck just enough to see her take her place at the front of the room. She's slender, lightly pierced, colourfully dressed with feathers in her hair.

"Hello everyone," she begins in a quiet, soothing voice. "Thank you all for coming and allowing me the privilege of guiding you through your practice this evening. Today, we're going to start seated at the front of our mats. Please make yourself comfortable in a cross-legged position. Keep your back straight, your neck slightly bent. And, when you're ready . . . close your eyes."

I scoot to the front of my mat and do as I am told.

"Place your hands open on your knees, palms up . . . Let all that beautiful energy flow into your palms and up through your forearms. Good . . . Breathe . . . Surrender to the present moment. If a thought enters your mind, gently acknowledge it and let it go. Picture it flying away like a delicate bird into a cloudless sky. It becomes a speck, and then there is nothing. Inhale deeply . . . Feel the air enter your nostrils and fill your lungs, giving you energy, vitality, strength. Exhale . . . Let go of any unnecessary tension . . . Inhale . . . Exhale . . . "

I try desperately to heal, to bring heat and relaxation to my loins.

"Beautiful. When you're ready, come into child's pose—*bālāsana*. Breathe deeply here, feeling your hips sinking toward your heels, feeling the gentle stretch through the upper back and the shoulders . . . We'll be holding this posture for two minutes . . . "

Slowly, we make our way through various poses, none of which cause me any substantial discomfort. When I enter pigeon pose, *kapotasana*, however, something goes terribly wrong. Without warning, the rear of my left testicle explodes with pain and agonizing jolts shoot up through my abdomen.

I let out a grunt and fall to my side.

The instructor seems not to notice. "Try to calm your mind," she continues. "Sink deeper into the posture.

Feel the negative energy leaving your glutes with each and every exhale. Surrender . . . Be present. You're exactly where you need to be . . . "

I climb onto my hands and knees and begin crawling towards the door, but a wave of nausea throws me down.

God . . . please . . .

Another wave. Another groan.

Dry heaving.

Help . . . God . . .

I struggle to move forward but slip on my own sweat. A second attempt amounts to nothing more than a pathetic squirm.

Please . . . I can't . . . I . . .

Suddenly, strong hands grab me about my ribs and yank me to my feet. Katie is there, too.

"I think I need to go to the hospital," I manage.

XV

THE PAIN SUBSIDES AFTER THAT INITIAL BURST, BUT THE area remains extraordinarily tender. The nausea, too, persists and, on top of everything, a dangerously high fever has emerged. Delirium is not far off.

Katie accompanies me to the hospital and remains there for about an hour or so before I finally convince her to leave. When we first arrive, the medical staff escorts me about—taking me to a number of different rooms, performing several minor tests, including an ultrasound.

While I'm having my arm pricked by needles, I overhear one of the doctors mumble something to a nurse about the ultrasound having ruled out the possibility of testicular torsion. "We'll just have to wait and see what the blood tests have to say," he concludes.

When I return to Katie, though, I lie and tell her that a twisted nut is precisely what they believe to be ailing me. Despite my high temperature, I have somehow remained lucid enough to cover myself. Before she leaves, I ask her not to say anything to Laura. "I'll tell her myself," I say.

After waiting alone for probably another hour or so as various individuals enter the hospital with conditions more pressing than my own, I am finally readmitted. The doctor explains that I am suffering from epididymitis. The infection is severe, and I need to take antibiotics intravenously until everything clears. Dr. Garrett had prescribed me an extremely low dose, which wasn't enough to kill the bacteria in my urethra. More than likely, an instance of retrograde ejaculation had also occurred and forced the infection deeper.

For fuck's sake.

I ask him if I suffer from anything other than a urinary tract infection and epididymitis. If the masseuse had transmitted one sickness, why not another? "What about crabs?" I ask. "Herpes? Syphilis? HIV?"

"Well, I can tell you that you do not have pubic louse. No syphilis, either. HSV and HIV are things that you can have your family doctor set up a test for. You should know, however, that, with HIV, antibodies might not show up until three months after infection—sometimes even six. And with an HSV test, although we can tell you if you're positive, we can't pinpoint where it's located, so it's not actually very useful. Most panels won't even look for it."

I groan. What the hell am I going to do about Laura

at Christmas? After so long apart, she'll be expecting sex during my visit later that month. Now, not only am I impotent due to pain, there's a chance I'm polluted as well. With any luck, she'll be on her period. We'll be busy, too—hopefully, too busy to find time to be alone. I suppose, if necessary, I can feign exhaustion or intoxication. Neither will be hard to believe during the holidays.

"Sir, I suggest that we get the first round in you right away. A nurse will be in to administer it shortly."

I look up at the doctor as he races out of the room, his uniform floating up behind him like a small, white cape.

"I'll be waiting," I mutter. "I'll be waiting."

XVI

I FINISH MY DAYS OF IV AND EAT ANOTHER ROUND OF ORAL antibiotics for good measure—this time, doxycycline. Although my pain has greatly decreased, it certainly hasn't vanished. The doctors assure me that the infection is gone and that the existence of some minor pain is nothing to worry about—that I should feel back to normal soon enough.

Despite their hopeful words, however, I remain unconvinced. This episode has caused me to lose faith in modern medicine. As a child, anytime I had been struck ill, medicine had saved me. Without fail, it had been quick and effective. Strep throat, bronchitis, otitis media. Yet, here I am—still in pain after having fed my body an enormous amount of drugs. Doctor Garrett had been wrong. Perhaps, the practitioners in the emergency ward, too, are not infallible. Or, maybe, whatever is ailing me is simply beyond their ability to kill or control. I've read online about super bacteria—antibiotic-resistant little devils who'll end the human race unless there's a timely breakthrough in the medical sciences.

Desperate for a full recovery, I quit my job at the supercentre. It didn't take long working there to realize that overnights are unhealthy, soul-sucking things. Michael doesn't say much when I tell him. Quite possibly, he's surprised I've even lasted as long as I have.

I keep on the natural remedies, too—the cranberry juice and garlic and coconut oil. Not yoga, of course. The very thought of a studio is like a taser to my nutsack.

Yet, I feel as though I still need to do more. I can't sit idly by as bacteria potentially colonizes my lower reaches. I need help. I need something beyond medicine, beyond science, beyond rest. I need to be touched, touched like Paul Edgecomb was touched by John Coffey.

Now, my experiences with psychedelics have caused me to think primarily as a pantheist. However, on Sunday, I resolve to attend Mass at the city's largest cathedral—a Catholic establishment and purported house of God the Father. My choice has little to do with doctrine or creed. I don't really care what those gathered believe. Any religious establishment would do so long as it looks stunning and isn't run by people who've forgotten how to act poetically—people who preach in suits and treat their sacred texts as though void of contradictions and written by the hand of God. No, in my circumstances, I need bearded men in flowing robes, hymns, and sacrifices. I need altars, holy water, and genuflection. I need healing. I need the beauty, the power, the mysterious magic of tried and true ritual proceedings. I need something that can give me hope . . .

THE church is exceptionally crowded. And being little more than punctual, I am forced to sit near the back—my view of the ceremony obstructed by a sea of heads nodding up and down like buoys on unsettled water. Fortunately, though, the cathedral has much else to entertain the eye. Stained-glass saints stand in each *tekhenu*-shaped window, meticulously painted murals decorate the vaulted ceiling, and mosaics cover every wall. The Stations of the Cross are depicted in finely carved stone and the chandeliers hang like flowers suspended in Heaven. The overall feeling is one of elation. Incense, fire, and song penetrate the spirit and force it up—higher—away from the body towards the thin, peaceful air above. I can see now why there was such fuss about drums entering the Church. Drums ground a person—connect one with the pulse of the earth, with the steady beating of one's own heart. The Church, however, seeks to facilitate a transcendental experience. Their god lives beyond the created world, past the rhythms of nature.

When the time comes, I join the other adherents in

communion despite having never participated before. In fact, I've never received any prior sacrament.

I suppose my actions are technically a sin, but the experience is wonderful nonetheless. The wine is sweet and gently warms my chest and stomach, and the wafer, transubstantiated or not, tastes unbelievable. I instantly lament the fact that grocery stores don't carry chip bags full of the stuff. A box of red wine and a bowl full of wafers and I'd rocket to Heaven's gate. Add a little gouda and I'd bust through its doors.

I file back into my pew, kneel down, and pray for healing as I try to imagine the sacrament in my stomach radiating subtle energy to my personal hell below. For the rest of Mass, I focus my mind in this way, not opening my eyes until the priest says, "The Mass is ended. Go now in peace to love and serve the Lord."

I meander about the cathedral while the rest of the congregation makes its lazy exit. The images of Christ's passion make me feel somewhat accompanied in my suffering. However, without even a single depiction of him receiving a low blow, a sense of unequivocal kinship is impossible.

I am just about ready to leave when I find myself unexpectedly drawn to a colourful display of candles near one of the exits. It brings to mind Chico Robas in a silent picture George and I had watched called *7th Heaven*. In the film, the going rate is five francs a candle and a wish with each. Chico lights two. With the first, he asks le bon Dieu for a promotion and, with the second, for a wife.

Chico gets both.

I drop a coin into the donation box and grab a stick to transfer fire to a new wick.

"Please, God," I whisper, "heal me before Christmas. Make me pain-free and clean again. If you do this, I will marry Laura and remain faithful for the rest of my days."

XVII

THE FAUCET IS SPRAYING EVERYWHERE—ALL OVER MY clothes and the kitchen floor. I twist the taps back and forth, fidget with the filter but receive only a face full of water.

For fuck's sake. How do I turn this damn thing off?

I kick the cupboard beneath the sink in frustration.

Maybe, I should just let the apartment flood. I great deluge would be fitting.

The cupboard pops open and reveals a red lever attached to the central pipe. I switch its direction. The water stops.

I decide not to call the landlord just yet. I'll let him know while I'm away. It's not that he isn't a pleasant enough fellow. He is. I just abhor the idea of property owners intruding on rented spaces. At least, if I'm not there, I can more easily put the matter out of my head.

I'll call tomorrow.

Unfortunately, this is not the only thing I'll have to do. Tomorrow is the twenty-third and that means the time has also come to face Laura. And, although I have been assured on a number of separate visits to the hospital that I harbour no bacterial infection, I'm still in pain.

And I am at a loss. God hasn't helped me like he helped Chico. And no one is able to provide a cause. Chronic pain, the doctor's all say. Chronic pain.

Chronic pain? That's not a proper fucking diagnosis. What about yeast? Varicose veins? What about prostatitis? Has anyone thought to check my prostate? No. Not even a single doctor has bothered to stick a quick finger up my ass to feel if the fucker is hard or squishy?

I throw some towels down onto the kitchen floor and open the fridge. That beer is still sitting there. Over a month without a single drop of alcohol. I crack it open and let it drain into the back of my throat. There'll be no avoiding drinking during the coming festivities. Might as well start a day early.

My hand squeezes the empty can into the shape of an hourglass. It tastes like more. But where to go?

Duck Son?

No, I don't think I can handle being near that massage parlour . . .

Nonsense. Cheap booze and you need to eat.

. . . . . .

Come on. Let's go.

. . . Alright . . . but only if I can order egg foo young.

APART from a small group of middle-aged suits spinning dishes back and forth on a lazy Susan, the restaurant is completely empty.

I sit near the back, gulping beer and eavesdropping on their conversation as I wait for my egg foo young.

"Actually, it's very useful," says one. "By the time you explain what it is, the mood's already gone."

"Wait, what's it called again?" asks another.

"A *gartel*. Most folks only wear theirs during prayer, but I wear mine all the time. It's proven its effectiveness, too. A few years back, I was helping cleanup after a social, and there was this beautiful Ukrainian woman..."

My egg foo young arrives, and I begin picking it apart with my chopsticks.

"... There was mutual attraction and we easily could have had intercourse..."

"Bullshit", blurts the man across from him.

"No, it's true. But, when I thought about having to explain my gartel, it just seemed like too much of a hassle. And, in the end, I went home and had great sex with my wife. You know, my father used to say, 'It doesn't matter where you get your appetite so long as you eat at home'."

"With my wife, I'd starve," jokes the man across the

table.

I continue tuning in and out for entertainment as I make quick work of the plate in front of me.

Finished, I drop both chopsticks onto the table, run two finger through the leftover gravy, and suck my digits dry.

Delicious. Why they don't turn those baskets of fries into poutines is beyond me . . .

The waitress comes with the bill. As usual, a fortune cookie sits on top.

I crack it open.

When a tortoise or piece of jade is injured in its repository—who's at fault?

"What are you trying to say? It's my fault?" I ask the paper in my hand.

Yes.

"My fault? It's not my fault. What choice did I have? I was manipulated. Biology. Environment. Nature. Nurture. Libido. Disney. Advertisements. I'm a victim!"

The choice was yours.

"Free will's an illusion! I'm a machine in a machine."

You were before the first cause.

"Fuck you."

WHEN I get back to the apartment that night, I toss and turn and pull at my hair like Felicitas does in

Clarence Brown's *Flesh and the Devil* as she wrestles with the thought of telling her husband the truth about her extramarital affair with his best friend, Leo.

You've gotta come clean with Laura.

Hell no! How many beers have you had tonight?

What other choice do you have?

Are you kidding me? There'd be tidal waves and fire.

Only for a moment. Then, you'd feel relief. The burden of your secret would disappear.

It'd destroy Laura—crush her ego, her romantic picture of the world . . .

That's true. Then, how about an old-fashioned breakup? Lord knows you fight enough. Act as if your trip to the massage parlour never happened.

During Christmas?! You monster . . .

What? Were you planning on being all fuzzy during the holidays? Don't prolong this.

. . . . . .

At the very least, move things in the right direction.

I'll see what I can do.

XVIII

HAVING A SHELTER, THE BUS STOP IS BETTER EQUIPPED than most in the city. However, on days like this one, I often feel that the thin, glass panes hovering a half foot above the ground are little more than a slap in the face. The shelter's orientation is also such that, if the red lights at the adjacent intersection are long enough and the wind just right, the doorless structure will fill with exhaust from the idling vehicles.

On this cold, dark morning, I half-hope for asphyxiation. What a blessing it would be not to have to enter the whirlwind of the coming days.

But I'm out of luck. The bus comes, and my lungs are still filling with air. I climb onboard and find a seat. Knowing that the trip will take about an hour and that the airport is the terminus, I try to sleep.

But to no avail.

Having drank the night before, I am, of course, exhausted. My winter parka, too, thick with duck feathers and rimmed with caribou fur, is wrapped about me and calling me to rest. The steady vibration of the bus's engine, though, and the unevenness of the road are vexing my genitals. No matter what I do, which position I try, I'm unable to lift my focus from the discomfort below.

The bus eventually comes to a halt at the airport. I hop off with a smoke pressed tightly between my lips. Best to have one or two before entering. Unexpected delays can easily turn an otherwise pleasant air-travel experience into a smoker's nightmare.

I check and recheck my pockets before going in. As a drug user, I enter these sorts of places cautiously. Tiny bits of drugs and paraphernalia have a way of sneaking up on a person, and we don't want to be responsible for ruining Christmas. I can picture it already—the arrest, the phone call, the story in my hometown paper . . .

When I get inside, I comb through my carry-on as well.

Just being in airports makes me nervous. Yet nothing quite compares to the process of going through security. Although innocent, I avoid eye contact with anyone in uniform as if I'm a fugitive. Even custodians bring my gaze to the floor. For whatever reason, the combination of those prying stares, security wands, metal detectors, and body scanners makes me feel as though I have a brick of cocaine up my ass.

Despite my insecure demeanour, however, I pass

through without issue and make it to my boarding gate with time to spare. Once seated on the aircraft, I again try to sleep. I'm still hungover and know a few hours of rest will go a long way. Besides, there's no point trying to stay awake for my choice of complementary coffee or apple juice. I mean, the scroogy sons of bitches aren't even doing a light snack anymore.

I doze off sometime during the safety demonstration and sleep straight through the flight. I don't recall take-off, and it isn't until the plane touches down that I'm finally jarred awake.

I'm to meet my parents at the usual spot—lot H, pillar seven. From there, we'll drive directly to their house to begin Christmas Eve dinner preparations. My mother will race back and forth between the kitchen and dinning room, and my father will get to work setting his bar in order. Every year, he completes his tasks with at least an hour to spare, and then pours my mother a glass of wine and himself an eggnog. Finally, he stations himself in the living room and stares at a televised fire until the first guest arrives. Most years, it's Uncle Rick.

As expected, I find my parents waiting in their SUV. I can see my mother through the window—wearing sunglasses and a bright spearmint-coloured coat. She has the mirror down and is shoving loose strands of hair back into her blonde bun.

It's my dad who sees me first. He seems to say

something to my mother as he opens the door, and she brings her hands down fast, accidentally switching on the hazard lights. They blink once or twice before she shuts them off and scrambles out of the vehicle.

I take quick steps towards her, arms spread wide for a hug. We are about to embrace when, suddenly, the rear, passenger-side door swings open.

Out steps Laura, grinning from ear to ear.

XIX

THE ENTIRE WAY TO MY PARENTS', LAURA KEEPS HER HAND on my leg, and, from time to time, nuzzles her head against my shoulder. Given the pain, presenting myself normally is somewhat of a challenge. But I do my best. Seeing my parents certainly helps. I even manage to smile a few times.

When we get home, my mother immediately sends me to shower with a fresh bar of soap. She claims that I smell of sweat and smoke and says she won't have her relations thinking I've been poorly raised.

I, of course, oblige. After all, she's correct. I smell exactly how she describes. Besides, I'm already itching to be alone, to be away from Laura.

I can't free myself of her entirely, however. As the water pours over me, my thoughts sway back and forth between her and my groin like a pendulum. I can picture her—joking with my dad, helping my mom in the kitchen. How many times has she been in this house since she started her internship?

And how will she react if she sees me in the nude? I look different—redder, veinier. I definitely don't function the same.

I climb out of the shower and dry off. I have to stop worrying.

Enjoy the holidays, Steven. Go get yourself a rum n' nog and watch the televised fire with your father.

THE guests trickle in—my grandmother first, and then Uncle Rick. Next comes Aunt Kim, Uncle Mark, and their four children. After that, a couple of my dad's cousins arrive with my grandmother's sister in tow. A few more stragglers follow and, by the time everyone is fixing their plates to eat, we're eighteen excited stomachs.

For the most part, everything proceeds smoothly. Gifts are exchanged, games are played, and I get to some serious drinking with Uncle Rick and my cousins. Laura, too, has her fair share of alcohol. The only minor hiccup in the evening is Grandma chocking on a piece of cheesecake. The whole gathering stops for a moment and gapes. Except for Aunt Kim, that is, who responds immediately, and, with a few well-placed slaps, dislodges the dessert and saves the party from ending catastrophically.

Laura and I offer to help clean up after the guests

have left, but my parents insist that we worry about it in the morning and usher us off to bed.

We agree and make our way downstairs to my old bedroom. Previously, the room's walls and furniture had been covered with posters and decals, and the air had reeked of sweat, mould, and spray deodorants. But, the moment I left home, my mother began redecorating. And, now, the walls are a tasteful, pumpkin-spice orange, and the room smells of freshly washed linens.

I shut the door behind us, and Laura immediately pounces on me, kissing my mouth. Not thinking, I kiss her back and begin removing her top. She reaches down to unbutton my pants.

And then, I remember myself.

"Fuck. Sorry, I gotta puke," I say, pushing Laura off me.

It's a lie, of course. But I rush to the bathroom anyway and hang my head over the toilet.

Laura walks in after me and rubs my back as I put on a quite a show—spitting, dry-heaving, curling my body about the porcelain like a scared, infant monkey in a Harry Harlow experiment.

By the time I'm done, there's no longer any talk of sex. In fact, there's no talk at all. Laura simply exits the washroom and goes to bed, leaving me alone to butt heads with my reflection.

XX

CHRISTMAS DAY IS TO BE SPENT WITH LAURA'S FAMILY, SO we shift houses at about noon and resume our merrymaking at her parent's place. I haven't been worried about any post-celebration matters. Laura's father won't allow us to sleep in the same room. He's of the opinion that sharing a bed is for married couples only. Clearly, he is opposed to Laura and I living together. Yet, to his credit, he never openly criticizes us. The most he ever does is emphasize the fact that our apartment has two bedrooms. Everything considered, him and I get along fine and, with the possibility of intercourse with his daughter off the table tonight, I'm relatively relaxed. In fact, I'm able to enjoy my drinks with the man more than usual.

The evening proceeds normally. Much like the night before, there's feasting and holiday cheer. Gifts are exchanged, although they're exchanged through some sort of Secret Santa mechanism I fail to understand. According to Laura's mother's instructions, several different bags and boxes make their way across my lap before, finally, I'm told to open the one in my possession. My own contribution is unknown to me. Laura has purchased something on my behalf.

I look around the room at the other guests as they excitedly rip open their presents and create fountains of giftwrap and ribbon.

"Well, aren't you going to open yours, Steven?" calls Laura's mother.

I consider the bag in front of me and grin drunkenly. Only a few sheets of coloured tissue paper stand between me and a new possession. I pick them out one by one and peak inside the bag.

You've gotta be fucking kidding me.

Massage oils.

My Secret Santa has bought me massage oils.

LONG after the party has ended, I find myself stretched out contentedly on a hide-a-bed in the basement—Laura safely a floor above. I'll be off tomorrow. The holiday season seems to have passed without issue.

I'm beginning to drift to sleep, the corners of my mouth raised in a slight smile, when, suddenly, I'm startled awake by something climbing onto the bed.

94

It's Laura.

She tears off the blankets and straddles me.

"Whoa," I say in a hushed voice. "What're you doin'? Your parents are upstairs."

"I don't care. We'll be quiet."

"I don't wanna piss off your dad on Christmas."

"We've done this a thousand times."

"I'm drunk and tired. Let's just go to bed."

She looks at me shrewdly. "We've been apart for four months, and you don't want to have sex with me? It's your last night."

"I'm just not feeling it . . . I'm tired."

"Bullshit. What's up?"

"Nothing."

"Tell me, Steven."

"Fuck. Nothing's up."

"Are you fucking another girl?!"

"God . . . "

"Are you?!"

"No. Chill out."

"Good. Then, we can have sex." Smiling, she reaches for my reproductive organ. But, as she makes contact, I wince. "What the fuck?!"

"It's nothing."

"What's wrong with your dick, Steven?"

"Nothing."

"Bullshit."

"Okay . . . I didn't wanna tell you. I twisted a ball last month, and it's still not right."

"Bullshit. Why didn't you tell me?"

"It's true. Katie took me to the hospital. You can ask her. I twisted it while doing yoga."

"Please don't tell me you're sleeping with Katie."

"She's celibate for fuck's sake. You can ask the whole damn yoga studio. Everyone saw me crawl outta there in pain."

"Why didn't you tell me?!" she whimpers.

"I didn't wanna worry you." I lie.

"Come on. Let me see."

"There's nothing to see. It just hurts, that's all.

She lets out a helpless groan and touches my face. "You can't look after yourself. You need me with you. Don't go back, Steven. Just stay here and don't work. Eat healthy. Get better."

"It's not a big deal," I assure her. "I should be back to normal in a couple of weeks. Don't worry, okay?"

"But I'm gonna miss you . . . " She scarcely gets out the words before beginning to cry, burying her face between my arm and my chest to muffle the sound. I cry, too, although my tears flow from a very different source.

We lie like this—silent, not saying another word until sleep takes its hold.

When I awake the following morning, the bed is empty. I'm alone; Laura is back upstairs.

XXI

DURING THE DAYS LEADING UP TO NEW YEAR'S EVE, I FALL into a pattern of late nights and later mornings fueled by drugs and alcohol. Without having to work, I have lost track of the date and am somewhat surprised when George phones and alerts me that it's already the thirty-first.

"So, you're commin' to Peter's art show?" he asks.

"Peter's art show?"

"Yeah . . . It's tonight."

Dammit.

I want very much to decline. I'm already half-drunk and comfortable with my rhythm. But the guy is dying and he'd thrown such an amazing party. How could I not go?

"Definitely," I say.

"Awesome. Get ready. I'll pick you up on the way."

\- - -

THE show is being held at a newly constructed gallery for the modern arts—a crescent-shaped building with an unreasonably long flight of stairs. Katie is already there when we arrive. She's standing near the entrance, talking with someone wearing a balaclava and smoking a joint. The two of them seem deep in conversation, so we simply give them a wave and enter the venue ourselves.

Inside, a host of red-faced individuals mingle about food-covered tables, chatting excitedly. And, to our delight, either side of the room is home to a wine bar. George and I leave our hats and jackets with coat check and each get ourselves a glass of pinot noir.

"Where's Peter?" I ask George.

"Not sure. Probably inside the show."

"Sure is," says a witchy-looking man beside him. "Peter is the show. You boys oughta get in there and check it out. I can confidently say it's his finest work to date." He smiles, plucks a pickle off the table, and places it onto his plate. "*The Last Stand* by Pierre Cote . . . Very powerful."

"Well, shall we?" asks George.

"Yeah. Just let me get one more glass of wine, and we'll go."

THE first room is square and silent. I was expecting paintings, but there are none. The entire room—walls, floor, and ceiling—has been painted black. In fact, the only colour in the room occurs at its center where a pile of brightly painted rubble lies illuminated.

I move in closer to inspect the heap. It consists of fruit-shaped pieces of concrete—bananas, apples, oranges—most of them broken, their rough, stony insides exposed.

George and I circle around the installation once or twice before continuing through the door at the back of the room. The portal opens to a dimly lit hallway, about fifty meters long, which slithers like a serpent. It's narrow, too—so narrow, in fact, that, if attendants were to move in opposite directions, they'd be forced to flatten themselves against the sides of the corridor just to squeeze past one another. It's certainly possible that a particularly plump individual would have no choice but to become contented circling about the fruit display.

The hall ends in a series of doors and short passages, which eventually open up into the final room—a giant, circular enclosure, painted white, flashing with strobe lights, and vibrating with trip hop. Hanging from the ceiling at eye-level are tens of thousands of tiny pictures of Peter, all of which have been chopped in two and painted red where they've been separated. The missing halves lie scattered and crimson about the floor.

I push past the photos to a clearing in the middle of the room. There's Peter—fat and naked, his whole body painted white, sitting in meditation. His face looks both peaceful and resolute, like that of a man about to conquer death.

I stare a moment longer before making my way to the exit.

By the time I return to the room housing the comestibles, George is no longer with me. We've become separated in the forest of photos. I walk past the food-covered tables in the direction of coat check.

I need a smoke.

Outside, there are several other smokers, including a group of young men chewing on cigars. They appear to be sharing their most revealing Freudian slips.

"The wife asked me what I was doin' in the kitchen," starts one. "I tried to say, 'I'm gettin' cranberry juice to wet my whistle', but, instead, I said, 'I need a guy named Wes to wet my noodle'!"

The group howls with laughter.

I light my cigarette and try to divorce my attention from their conversation, focusing my thoughts, instead, on Laura. I need to deal with this issue once and for all.

If Peter can die with such power and grace, surely I can find the strength to kill this relationship. I have to. And not just because of my balls. For many reasons, I have to. There's no other way. I have to kill it.

But, before I can consider how, my mediation is cut short by shouts from the cigar-smoking men. A person has burst through the gallery doors and is now tumbling headlong down the stairs to the street below.

The individual comes to a halt about midway—sprawled out, limbs mangled.

I wait for a moment. But there's no movement. No effort whatsoever.

Instinctively, I race down the steps to offer what aid I can.

As I approach the body, it becomes clear the person is wearing a balaclava. Blood leaks out from the material and, in the lamplight, appears to spread like a shadow across the snow.

I pull off the mask, and my eyes grow wide.

The face is Kelly's.

Epilogue

SIX MONTHS LATER, I'M LOUNGING IN MY NEW APARTMENT, watching *Un chien andalou*. The sun is beating in, slowly melting my iced cappuccino, and, on the screen, Luis Buñuel is running a razor through Simone Mareuil's eye.

A short while later, she is further molested by a young Pierre Batcheff.

It are at times like these that I pause and think about all that had happened.

Kelly had died that night, not from the fall but from the brain aneurism that preceded it.

My relationship with Laura had died that night as well, although, admittedly, it had taken a few more weeks to finally muster up the courage to call it off and some months after that to completely pull it apart. Throughout the entire process, Peter's show had provided me with strength. There had, of course, been tears, relapses, fighting. But, every time I thought back to his naked, terminally ill body sitting firmly at the center of that room, it renewed my resolve, and I was able to proceed one step further down the path to breakup.

By the time I turn my attention back to the film in front of me, Mareuil is walking arm in arm down a rocky beach with another man. It seems that, after all that nightmarish chaos, she's finally found peace.

Or, maybe, not.

A title card appears, which reads, "au printemps", and is followed by an image of the couple half-buried in sand, presumably dead—their heads positioned oddly as if awaiting decay.

I suppose this is the way of things. Ups. Downs. Cycles of tears and laughter—only the best among us wise enough to search for the goddamn hub.

Suddenly, pain shoots through my epididymis.

Ice! I need some ... iced cappuccino ...

I press the sweating cup tight to my scrotum and sigh.

I think it's time I watched something in colour.

www.ingramcontent.com/pod-product-compliance
Lightning Source LLC
Chambersburg PA
CBHW020744130626
46554CB00006B/2148